Beauty and the Beast

and other stories

Miles
Kelly

First published in 2011 by Miles Kelly Publishing Ltd
Harding's Barn, Bardfield End Green, Thaxted, Essex, CM6 3PX, UK

Copyright © Miles Kelly Publishing Ltd 2011

This edition printed 2013

2 4 6 8 10 9 7 5 3

Publishing Director Belinda Gallagher
Creative Director Jo Cowan
Editor Amanda Askew
Senior Designer Joe Jones
Production Manager Elizabeth Collins
Reprographics Anthony Cambray, Stephan Davis, Lorraine King, Jennifer Hunt
Assets Lorraine King

ISBN 978-1-84810-496-9

Printed in China

British Library Cataloguing-in-Publication Data
A catalogue record for this book is available from the British Library

ACKNOWLEDGEMENTS
Artworks are from the Miles Kelly Artwork Bank

Cover artwork by Frank Endersby (Beehive Illustration)

Every effort has been made to acknowledge the source and copyright holder of each picture.
Miles Kelly Publishing apologises for any unintentional errors or omissions.

Made with paper from a sustainable forest

www.mileskelly.net
info@mileskelly.net
www.factsforprojects.com

Contents

Beauty and the Beast

Retold from the original tale by
Madame Leprince de Beaumont

THERE WAS ONCE a businessman who had made a fortune by trading overseas. He lived in a magnificent mansion staffed by servants and with a TV in every room – including the indoor swimming pool. The businessman's wife had died, so he had brought up their three beautiful daughters on his own.

Unfortunately, the two eldest girls, Bianca and Bettina, lazed about all day watching chat shows, flicking through magazines and day-dreaming of marrying professional footballers. But Belle, the youngest daughter, was a great help to her father in running his business. She also enjoyed reading books on engineering and space exploration, for she was as intelligent as she was beautiful, and she had an avid interest in rocket science.

The businessman once had to go away on an important trip for work.

"Don't forget to bring us back some jewellery!" yelled Bianca.

"And some perfume!" bellowed Bettina.

"Is there nothing you would like, darling?" the businessman asked Belle.

Belle thought for a while. "Just a beautiful rose, please Daddy," she smiled.

"That's my girl!" the businessman said, and gave a cheery wave as he drove away.

But when the businessman finally returned, he was downcast and empty-handed.

"I'm afraid your dear old Dad has had it," the businessman explained. "I was on my way back last night, but it was dark and raining and somehow I got completely lost in the middle of nowhere. The only house for miles around was a spooky old mansion, and I went to ask for help. The lights were on, the front door was open, but nobody seemed to be at home. I thought it was very strange, but I was so desperate that I crept inside and stayed the night. Early this morning, as I was hurrying off through the grounds, I stopped to pick a rose for Belle. 'STOP THIEF!' someone roared. 'This is my house and those are my roses! Is this how you repay my hospitality? I am going to kill you!' The man who came striding towards me was uglier than a monster in a film. He had a hairy face and bloodshot eyes, a snout for a nose and teeth like fangs. His hands were clawed and his body huge and hulking. I realised that the beast was deadly serious, so I fell on my knees in terror and begged for mercy. 'I will give you three months to say goodbye to everyone,' he growled. 'After that, you must return here to die... unless you have a daughter who is willing to come in your place and live here with me forever.'"

Bianca and Bettina stood gawping in horror. "Oh Daddy," they wailed, "who is going to look after us when you're gone?"

"Don't worry, Daddy," Belle comforted her father. "I can't let you die. I will go instead of you."

"Belle, you will do nothing of the kind!" her father protested. "You haven't seen this guy!"

"I don't care!" said Belle, resolutely sticking out her chin. And nothing Belle's father could say would make her change her mind. "If you sneak off without me, I shall just follow you," was her final word on the subject. So three months later, the broken-hearted businessman accompanied his brave daughter to the door of the huge, lonely mansion and kissed her for the last time. He could hardly see through his tears as he turned and walked away...

"Right," Belle said to herself firmly, though her bottom lip was trembling. "Let's find the library. Maybe it has a good science section." She set off through the stone corridors and oak-panelled halls, exploring. It was an eerie feeling to be all alone in such an enormous old place. Suddenly, Belle stopped in surprise. There, right in front of her was a door marked 'Belle's room'. She put her hand on the iron handle and gently pushed. It swung open with a creak. Belle gasped with delight. Inside, was everything she could possibly have wished for. There was a soft, white bed. Wardrobes full of beautiful clothes. But best of all, lining the walls was shelf after shelf of books.

"The owner of this place can't be all bad," Belle murmured to herself. She drew down the nearest book. It was bound in ancient leather and had gold-edging.

She read the first page:

> Belle, you have a heart of gold
> Like girls in fairytales of old.
> Whatever you wish, it will come true
> There's magic waiting here for you.

"Hmmm," wondered Belle. "Well, the only thing I really wish is that I could see if my Dad is okay."

At that very moment, Belle noticed a mirror on the bedroom wall begin to cloud over. Mists swirled across the glass, and when they cleared, instead of her own reflection, she saw a picture of her father, sitting at home sadly without her. After a few moments the picture vanished, but Belle was very grateful to have been able to see her father at all. *The owner of this place is actually very kind,* Belle thought to herself.

Just then, Belle heard the dinner bell ringing from the great hall. She hurried along and found a delicious meal laid out for one. No sooner had she swallowed three mouthfuls than she heard a shuffling and a snuffling. The food stuck in her throat and her heartbeat quickened. Belle forced herself to turn round and face her host.

Her father had been right. He was truly hideous.

"I'm Belle," she whispered, remembering her manners, like the well-brought up girl she was. "My room is wonderful – thank you."

"Call me Beast," said the monster, a look of pleasure lighting up his sad eyes. "Did you really like everything?"

"Yes, of course," said Belle. "Particularly the books. I love books, especially those on rocket science."

"They are your books now," said Beast. "Everything here is yours. I give it all to you. You can do with everything just what you wish. That goes for me, too. If I'm bothering you just tell me to go away and I will."

The Beast looked down at his huge, flat feet. "I know I'm exceedingly ugly. I might put you off your food." He sighed. "And not only am I ugly, I'm very stupid too."

"Now, now," comforted Belle. "I'm sure that's not the case. Anyone who is ready to say they are stupid can't possibly be stupid. The only people who really are stupid are those who won't admit that they're stupid!"

"Do you really think so?" sighed the Beast.

"Yes, of course!" laughed Belle. "And if you're really worried about being stupid, I can teach you all about rocket science. Let me get my books..."

A sheepish smile came over the Beast's ugly face as he listened to Belle read. After a while, he suddenly interrupted her.

"Belle, will you marry me?" he asked.

Belle was extremely taken aback. She looked at the monster as he crouched adoringly in front of her. "I'm sorry," she said. "I wish I could, but I really don't want to."

And so the time passed. Each day, Belle read in her room and walked in the beautiful grounds, admiring the roses. And each evening, the Beast came to visit her. As the weeks went on, Belle began to enjoy his company and looked forward to seeing him. But each night the Beast asked her to marry him, and even though Belle liked him more and more as a friend, she simply couldn't – well, fancy him.

Belle's only other worry was her Dad. Each day she saw in the mirror that he was pining more and more without her. Her sisters were selfish, unkind and thoughtless, and her father had grown quiet and pale and thin.

"Dear Beast," Belle begged one night, "allow me to go back to see my dad. I am afraid that he is dying of a broken heart."

Much to Belle's surprise, the Beast nodded his agreement. "Of course, Belle," he said, "if that is what will make you happy. Only I don't know what I'll do without you..."

"Darling Beast," whispered Belle, stroking his matted, shaggy hair, "I promise I'll be back in a week."

"Then I promise you that when you wake up tomorrow morning, you'll be at home with your father," sighed the Beast. "Take this ring. When you're ready to leave, just put it by the side of your bed at night. As you sleep, it will bring you back here."

Sure enough, next morning Belle woke up back in her old bed. Her dad couldn't believe his eyes! He and Belle hugged and laughed and spent a wonderful holiday doing all the things they used to enjoy doing together – going through his accounts, visiting the science museum, watching old musicals on TV... The week flew by in the twinkling of an eye. "Please, Belle, don't go," begged her dad, and Belle didn't have the heart to leave.

But several nights later, Belle had a terrible dream. She saw the Beast lying in the garden of his mansion, under the rose bushes that he loved so much.

Belle knew that he was dying.

"Daddy," she sobbed the next morning. "I'm worried that something dreadful has happened to the Beast. He's my best and truest friend – and it's all my fault!"

That night, Belle put the Beast's ring by her bedside. It didn't seem as if she'd been asleep for five minutes when she woke up in her beautiful white room in the mansion. Belle sped off into the moonlit garden and there, lying under the rose bushes just as in her dream, lay the Beast. She flung herself down by his side and heaved his big, heavy head into her lap. Her tears plopped one by one onto his hairy face.

Weakly, the Beast opened his eyes and smiled. "I thought you had forgotten your promise," he whispered. "Now I have seen you once again, I can die happily."

"No!" Belle cried. "You can't die! You mustn't leave me! I love you!" And she kissed him.

At that very moment, the night sky was lit up by a million rainbow-coloured fireworks. Belle gazed upwards in surprise – she thought things like that only happened in films. When she looked back down at the Beast again, the monster was gone. Lying in her lap was a handsome, happy prince. He sprang up and lifted

Belle to her feet with joy in his eyes.

"My darling Belle," he told her, "Thank you for setting me free! I have lived under a wicked enchantment for years which forced me to appear as the Beast – not only ugly but stupid, too – until a beautiful girl willingly fell in love with me. You are the only person in the world who saw through my ugly appearance and sensed what I was really like inside. Now we will live together happily forever."

And that's exactly what they did. But this is a real tale, not a fairytale, and real tales don't have entirely happy endings. The prince took

Belle to live at his palace – and her dad went to live with them too. But Belle's selfish sisters got what they deserved. They were turned into statues and set at the palace gates until such time as they began to think about other people rather than themselves. As far as I know, they're both there still…

Cinderella

Retold from the original tale
by Charles Perrault

ONCE UPON A TIME, when there were still fairy godmothers, there was a girl called Cinderella. She lived with her father and his new wife, and her two new step-sisters. The step-mother did not like Cinderella very much, mostly because she was so much nicer than her own two daughters. Cinderella was also much prettier. Oh, but the step-sisters were ugly!

Cinderella had to do all the work in the house as the ugly sisters were also very lazy. They spent all the father's money on new clothes and endless pairs of shoes, and then went off to parties leaving poor Cinderella with piles of stockings to mend.

One day a very grand invitation arrived. The prince

was looking for a wife, and had decided to give a ball in three days time for all the young ladies in the land. The ugly sisters could talk about nothing else. They bought lots of new dresses and many pairs of matching shoes, and then spent every hour trying them all on.

They made Cinderella curl their hair and iron their ribbons and powder their noses. Cinderella was so exhausted running around after them that she had no time to look into her own wardrobe to choose what she should wear.

In a waft of perfume, the ugly sisters swept out of the door into the carriage without as much as a thank you to Cinderella. She closed the door sadly, and went to sit by the fire in the kitchen.

"I wish I could have gone to the ball, too," she sighed.

There was a sudden swirl of stars, and there in front of Cinderella stood an old lady with a twinkle in her eye, and a wand in her hand.

"You shall go to the ball, my dear Cinderella. I am your fairy godmother," she said, smiling. "Now, we must be quick, there is much to do! Please bring me a large pumpkin from the vegetable patch. Oh, and six mice from the barn, and you will find four lizards by the water butt."

Cinderella did as she was bid. With a wave of the wand, the pumpkin was turned into a glittering golden coach and the mice into six pure white horses. The lizards became elegant footmen, dressed in green velvet.

"Now you, my dear," said the fairy godmother, turning to Cinderella. A wave of the wand, and Cinderella's old apron disappeared and there she stood in a white dress, glittering with golden stars. Her hair was piled on top of her head and it too was sprinkled with stars. On her feet were tiny glass slippers with diamonds in the heels.

"Enjoy yourself, my dear," said the fairy godmother, "but you must leave before midnight for then my magic ends and you will be back in your old apron with some mice and lizards at your feet!"

When Cinderella arrived at the ball everyone turned to look and stare at this unknown beauty who had arrived so unexpectedly. The prince hurried over to

ask her to dance and then would not dance with anyone else all evening. The ugly sisters were beside themselves with rage, which of course made them look even uglier.

Cinderella was enjoying herself so much that she forgot the fairy godmother's warning, so she had a terrible fright when the clock began to strike midnight. She turned from the prince with a cry and ran down the stairs of the palace into her carriage, and disappeared as suddenly as she had arrived. One of the tiny glass slippers with diamonds sparkling in the heels had slipped from her foot as she ran. The prince picked it up and turning to the crowded ballroom declared, "I shall marry the girl whose foot fits this slipper!"

Cinderella, meanwhile, had just managed to reach her garden gate when all her finery disappeared, and by the time the ugly sisters arrived home, both in a towering rage, she was sitting quietly by the fire.

The next morning, the prince went from house to house looking for the mystery girl whose foot would fit the glass slipper. But no one had feet that small. He reached Cinderella's house where first one ugly sister and then the next tried to squash her big feet into the slipper.

"Please let me try," said a quiet voice from the corner, and Cinderella stepped forward. The sisters just laughed in scorn but they soon stopped when they saw that the tiny slipper fitted Cinderella perfectly. There was a sudden swirl of stars, and there in front of Cinderella stood her fairy godmother with a twinkle in her eye, and a wand in her hand. In an instant, Cinderella was clothed in a gorgeous dress of cornflower blue silk decorated with pearls. On her feet she wore white boots with blue tassels.

The prince whisked Cinderella off to the palace to meet the king and queen, and the wedding took place the very next day. Cinderella forgave the ugly sisters, she was that sort of girl. But the prince insisted the sisters spent one day a week working in the palace kitchens just to remind them how horrid they had been to Cinderella.

Snow White and Rose Red

Retold from the original story by the Brothers Grimm

ONCE UPON A TIME there was a widow who had two daughters, Snow White and Rose Red. Snow White was quiet and gentle, Rose Red was wild as the hills, but they loved each other, and their mother, so the little house in the woods was a happy one.

One winter evening as they all sat round the fire there was a knock at the door. Rose Red opened it and gave a scream. There stood a great big brown bear! But in a deep rumbly voice the bear said, "Please do not be afraid. All I ask is that you let me sleep by your fire tonight. It is so cold outside."

"Of course you may shelter with us," said the mother. And she called the girls to set the soup on the stove and to put another log on the fire.

"Would you brush the snow from my fur, please?" asked the bear. Rose Red fetched the big broom and carefully brushed the bear's great shaggy coat. Snow White gave him a great bowl of hot soup and the bear gulped it down in one. Then he stretched out in front of the fire and was soon fast asleep.

In the morning, Snow White let him out of the

cottage and he padded off into the forest through the deep snow. But in the evening, he returned and once again Snow White and Rose Red and their mother looked after him. After that the bear came every night all through the winter, and they grew very fond of him. But when spring came, the bear told them he would not be returning any more.

"I have to guard my treasure. Once the snows have melted all kinds of wicked people try to steal it," he said and giving them all a hug he set off through the forest. Just as he passed through the garden gate, his fur caught on a nail. For a fleeting moment Snow White thought she saw a glint of gold, but the bear hurried off and was soon out of sight.

A few days later, Rose Red and Snow White were out gathering berries to make jam when they came alongside a fallen tree. Then they saw a very cross dwarf, tugging at his beard which was trapped by the great tree trunk.

"Well, don't stand there like a pair of silly geese! Come and help me!" he shrieked.

Well, no matter how hard they tugged, Rose Red and Snow White were not strong enough

to lift the tree, so Rose Red took her scissors out and snipped off the end of the dwarf's beard. He was absolutely furious, and snatched up a big bag of gold from the tree roots and disappeared without a word of thanks.

Some days later the girls' mother said she really fancied a piece of fish for supper, so they went down to the river to see what they could catch. But instead of a fish, there on the bank they found the cross dwarf again. This time his beard was caught up in his fishing line.

"Don't just stand there gawping," he yelled, "help me get free!"

Snow White tried to untangle it but it was impossible, so she too snipped a piece off his beard. He was quite white with rage, but just grasped a casket of jewels that lay at the water's edge and turned away without a word of thanks.

It was the Spring Fair a few days later. The girls

decided to go and buy some new ribbons for their hats, and their mother wanted needles for her embroidery, so they set off early in the morning. They had not gone far when they heard a terrible shrieking and crying. They ran towards the sound, and there once more was the cross dwarf, this time struggling in the huge talons of an eagle. They tugged and tugged and the eagle had to let go.

"You have torn my coat," muttered the ungrateful dwarf and picked up a basket of pearls and hobbled off as fast as possible. The girls just laughed and continued on their way to the fair.

They had a wonderful time, and it was quite late when they walked slowly home. The sun was just sinking behind a big rock when, to their astonishment, they came across the dwarf again. There, spread out on the ground in front of him, was a great pile of gold, precious jewels and pearls.

Suddenly the dwarf saw Snow White and Rose Red.

"Go away! Go away! You horrid girls are always in my way," he shouted. But just then there was a huge growl and the great brown bear stood by their side. With one huge paw he swiped the dwarf up, up into the sky and no one ever saw where he fell to earth again. The bear turned towards Snow White and Rose Red and as they looked, his great shaggy coat fell away. There stood a handsome young man, dressed in a golden suit of the richest velvet.

"Do not be afraid, Snow White and Rose Red," he said smiling. "Now you can see who I really am. That wicked dwarf put a spell on me so he could steal all my treasure, but you have broken the spell by your kindness."

They all went home, laden with the treasure. They talked long into the night, and it was all still true the next morning! Snow White married the handsome young man who, by great good fortune, had a younger brother who married Rose Red, so they all lived happily ever after.

So if you ever find a dwarf with half his beard missing, I would be very careful if I were you.

The Fish and the Ring

By Flora Annie Steel

ONCE UPON A TIME there lived a baron who was a great magician, and could tell by his arts and charms everything that was going to happen at any time.

Now this great lord had a little son born to him as heir to all his castles and lands. So, when the little lad was about four years old, wishing to know what his fortune would be, the baron looked in his Book of Fate to see what it foretold.

And, lo and behold! It was written that this much-loved, much-prized heir to all the great lands and castles was to marry a low-born maiden. So the baron was dismayed, and set to work by more arts and charms to discover if this maiden were already born, and if so, where she lived.

And he found out that she had just been born in a very poor house, where the poor parents already had five children.

So he called for his horse and rode far away, until he came to the poor man's house, and there he found the poor man sitting at his doorstep very sad and doleful.

"What is the matter, my friend?" asked he, and the poor man replied:

"May it please your honour, a little lass has just been born to our house, and we have five children already, and where the bread is to come from to fill the sixth mouth, we know not."

"If that be all your trouble," said the baron readily, "maybe I can help you. So don't be downhearted. I am just looking for such a little lass to be a companion to my son, so, if you will, I will give you ten crowns for her."

Well! The man he nigh jumped for joy, since he was to get good money, and his daughter, so he thought, a good home. Therefore he brought out the child then and there, and the baron, wrapping the babe in his cloak, rode away. But when he got to the river he flung the little thing into the swollen stream, and said to himself as he galloped back to his castle:

"There goes Fate!"

But, you see, he was just sore mistaken. For the little lass didn't sink. The stream was very swift, and her long clothes kept her up till she caught in a snag just opposite a fisherman, who was mending his nets.

Now the fisherman and his wife had no children, and they were just longing for a baby, so when the good man saw the little lass he was overcome with joy, and took her home to his wife, who received her with open arms.

And there she grew up, the apple of their eyes, into the most beautiful maiden that ever was seen.

Now, when she was about fifteen years of age, it so happened that the baron and his friends went a-hunting along the banks of the river and stopped to get a drink of water at the fisherman's hut. And who should bring the water out but, as they thought, the fisherman's daughter.

The young men of the party noticed her beauty, and one of them said to the baron, "She should marry well, read us her fate, since you are so learned in the art."

Then the baron, scarce looking at her, said carelessly, "I could guess her fate! Some wretched yokel or other. But, to please you, I will cast her horoscope by the stars, so tell me, girl, what day you were born?"

"That I cannot tell, sir," replied the girl, "for I was picked up in the river about fifteen years ago."

Then the baron grew pale, for he guessed at once that she was the little lass he had flung into the stream, and that Fate had been stronger than he was. But he kept his own counsel and said nothing at the time. Afterwards, however, he thought out a plan, so he rode back and gave the girl a letter.

"See you!" he said. "I will make your fortune. Take this letter to my brother, who needs a good girl, and you will be settled for life."

Now the fisherman and his wife were growing old and needed help, so the girl said she would go, and took the letter.

And the baron rode back to his castle saying to himself once more:

"There goes Fate!"

For what he had written in the letter was this:

Dear Brother, take the bearer and put her to death immediately.

But once again he was sore mistaken, since on the way to the town where his brother lived, the girl had to stop the night in a little inn. And it so happened that that very night a gang of thieves broke into the inn, and not content with carrying off all that the innkeeper possessed, they searched the pockets of the guests, and found the letter which the girl carried. And when they read it, they agreed that it was a mean trick and a shame. So their captain sat down and, taking pen and paper, wrote instead:

Dear Brother, take the bearer and marry her to my son without delay.

Then, after putting the note into an envelope and sealing it up, they gave it to the girl and bade her go on her way. So when she arrived at the brother's castle, though rather surprised, he gave orders for a wedding feast to be prepared. And the baron's son, who was staying with his uncle, seeing the girl's great beauty, was not unwilling, so they were fast wedded.

Well! When the news was brought to the baron, he was beside himself, but he was determined not to be outdone by Fate. So he rode quickly to his brother's and pretended to be quite pleased. And then one day, when no one was near, he asked the young bride to come for a walk with him, and when they were close to some cliffs, seized hold of her, and was for throwing her over into the sea. But she begged hard for her life.

"It is not my fault," she said. "I have done nothing. It is Fate. But if you will spare my life I promise that I will fight against Fate also. I will never see you or your son again until you desire it. That will be safer for you, since, see you, the sea may preserve me, as the river did."

Well! The baron agreed to this. So he took off his gold ring from his finger and flung it over the cliffs into the sea and said:

"Never dare to show me your face again till you can show me that ring likewise."

And with that he let her go.

Well! The girl wandered on, and she wandered on, until she came to a nobleman's castle, and there, as they needed a kitchen girl, she took work.

Now one day, as she was cleaning a big fish, she looked out of the kitchen window, and who should she see driving up to dinner but the baron and his young son, her husband. At first she thought that, to keep her promise, she must run away, but afterwards she remembered they would not see her in the kitchen, so she went on with her cleaning of the big fish.

And, lo and behold! She saw something shine in its inside, and there, sure enough, was the baron's ring! She was glad enough to see it, I can tell you, so she slipped it on to her thumb. But she went on with her work, and dressed the fish as nicely as ever she could, and served it up as pretty as may be, with parsley sauce and butter.

Well! When it came to table the guests liked it so well that they asked the host who cooked it. And he called to his servants, "Send up the cook who cooked that fine fish, that she may get her reward."

Well! When the girl heard she was wanted she made herself ready, and with the gold ring on her thumb, went boldly into the dining hall. And all the guests when they saw her were struck dumb by her wonderful beauty. And the young husband started up gladly, but the baron, recognizing her, jumped up angrily and looked as if he would kill her. So, without one word, the girl held up her hand before his face, and the gold ring shone and glittered on it, and she went straight up to the baron, and laid her hand with the ring on it before him on the table.

Then the baron understood that Fate had been too strong for him, so he took her by the hand, and, placing her beside him, turned to the guests and said:

"This is my son's wife. Let us drink a toast in her honour."

And after dinner he took her and his son home to his castle, where they all lived as happy as could be forever afterwards.